AF265930

RUTH STOCKHOUSE

AuthorHouse™
1663 Liberty Drive, Suite 200
Bloomington, IN 47403
www.authorhouse.com
Phone: 1-800-839-8640

First published by AuthorHouse   9/12/2008

ISBN: 978-1-4343-8902-2 (sc)

Library of Congress Control Number: 2008904820

Printed in the United States of America
Bloomington, Indiana

This book is printed on acid-free paper.

After six innings at Wrigley Field, the score between the Houston Astros and the Chicago Cubs was tied, 2 - 2. It was an extremely hot and humid afternoon and by that time the starting pitchers for the teams became fatigued and heated and thus less effective. They were two older pitchers and their match up was promoted as a duel of sorts and so it was for two-thirds of the game but then they were taken out and the duties fell to the relief pitchers for the final three innings.

The game began to change and wilt around the edges, errors were made by both teams, easy hits slipped through the infield just out of reach of flanking players and, oddly, both right fielders lost the ball in the sun and it dropped for hits. Fortunately, the sluggish playing did not result in additional runs for either team, a tribute to good pitching in the seventh and eighth innings.

To the ninth inning, however, as they might say, the tide turned. A wild pitch by the Cubs and a throwing error gave the Astros the best chance of going ahead. Their first batter had gotten an infield hit but moved to second base on the wild pitch and throw. The next batter made a sacrifice flyout but the flying runner got to third. Tensions mounted but were eased when the next batter struck out. Then a pinch hitter was sent in for the Astros. A hefty looking man he was and he took two mighty swings and missed. But then another swing he took and a definite crack could be heard and it was an explosion that sent the ball towering over the left field grandstand and onward somewhere to the street below. A home run it was and the last hurrah for the Cubs as they did not score in their half of the ninth and lost 4 - 2.

The custodian in charge of the parking lot below the outfield stands was the first to see the body. It was laying along side the only car remaining and was the reason for the custodian to approach and question why it was still there. At first, he was shocked and stared in disbelief at the man laying down with the left cheek in a pool of blood and his arms outstretched on each side as if the only maneuver possible from the jolt that had hit him. The right side of his face was strangely smooth and nothing leaked from it but it seemed to the custodian like a baloon that had been deflated. Flies were already hovering around the head and a faint, bad odor was coming forth.

The custodian regained his senses and called the police and the force was on the spot led by Lieutenant Watson. They roped off the area and their bustling moves brought forth a ring of surprised and curious spectators, apparently last stragglers from the ball park.

One astute observer, surveying the scene, eagerly approached Lieutenant Watson and identified the body.

"He's the camera man," the astute one said. "I saw him earlier taking pictures."

"Camera man?" queried Lieutenant Watson as he quickly reached for his pen and notepad.

"Sure," the helper went on, "inside the park, taking pictires for the TV station."

As the helper gave forth the man's name and TV address to Lieutenant Watson who listed them and then thought, ah, how good when civilians do their job and what a 'thank you' it was to get an immediate identification of the body.

Blessings for Lieutenant Watson did not cease, however, when a skinny fellow, with shirt open and wearing a large straw hat, slowly pushed his way forward. Lieutenant Watson saw him coming and noticed that others gave the man clear passage and Lieutenant Watson believed it was the definite odor of beer about him that almost subdued Lieutenant Watson when he stood before him.

"I saw somebody here," the man said in a shaky voice and a large gulp.

Lieutenant Watson sniffed and held his breath but stood his ground with his pen poised over his notepad.

Thinking that Lieutenant Watson wanted him to go on, the fellow obliged.

"It was someone here, he was walking and carrying a violin case. I saw him from the upper grand stand where I had my seat and I looked because I was following that home run ball as it flew across the street and landed somewhere. That is when I saw him here."

Lieutenant Watson's enthusiasm vanished for civilian cooperation and he did not write,

Unbelievingly, he asked, "A violin case, you say?"

"Yeah," the man answered sternly and stiffened his posture. "He was walking here, had a big hat on his head, and carried a violin case."

Lieutenant Watson obligingly wrote down the man's name and address and his story, thanked him without sincerity and said that he could leave.

By this time the medics were on the scene. The chief medical officer was officially responsible for declaring the man dead and for making speculation as to the possible time. His statement gave the cause of death resulted from several severe blows to the back of the victim's head. Although he was certain his evaluation would be confirmed by an autopsy, he added that he would be more precise after an autopsy. After taking the temperature of the corpse, he said only that the time was recent, perhaps between one or two hours ago or about the time the baseball game ended. He would say no more than the weapon was some sort of heavy object, either metal or wood, and probably smooth with no rough edges. The body was then photographed and taken to the morgue.

Though not in the official report, it should be noted that before the baseball game, 10,000 miniature Louisville Slugger bats were given away.

Lieutenant Watson returned to the precinct to record his report on the slaying of the camera man. This notable exercise was given to Scooter, a young officer seated at the next desk and presently assigned to paper work in the Homicide Division but awaiting promotion equivalent to experience as gained.

Lieutenant Watson liked giving an oral report also and he recited loudly as if to proclaim his expertness in the case.

"I spoke to two witnesses," he stated and acknowledged the one who identified the body and his name and address were duly noted. He saw that Scooter smiled and nodded his head in approbation as he was taking it all down on paper.

Lieutenant Watson smiled too and emitted a slight laugh before he continued.

"Another witness came forward to report seeing a person at the scene walking away carrying a violin case."

He paused and awaited a questionable response from Scooter, but Scooter's countenance did not change and he wrote the words without discretion.

The silence continued for a moment then Scooter said, with nonchalance, "That sounds like Seymour."

The smile vanished front Lieutenant Watson's face and he stared at Scooter.

"You know him?" he asked. "This fellow?"

"Well," Scooter replied, "not the witness, no; but the one carrying the violin case. He is Seymour."

Disbelief was full upon Lieutenant Watson and he continued his stare at Scooter.

"You said 'Seymour'", he stated. "Who is that?"

Scooter answered with causualness, unchanged by Lieutenant Watson's sudden sharp remarks.

"Seymour is one of those street musicians. I've seen him outside the field many times, playing his violin." Aware of the silence again, Scooter felt obliged to continue, "These musicians play around the city, you know, not only at Wrigley Field, but places like the Michigan Avenue bridge and the train station at Randolph and Michigan." Now Scooter stopped and laughed. "The joke about them is that they play to large audiences."

Lieutenant Watson sat quietly, not saying any more, perhaps not yet aware that the probable killer had been identified. However two things might be said for him:

Lieutenant Watson had no interest in music or baseball. Whatever interests might exist in between is a guess.

Nevertheless, the following day, Lieutenant Watson was at Wrigley Field and talking to the street musicians. The first group he approached were the gents with brass instruments. They looked at him skeptically when he asked, "Do you know Seymour?"

The musicians did not reply immediately, pondering the inquiry as they looked at one another; then in similar answers said, "Sure, we know Seymour. A really good violin player, here all the time." As these words were given out, their feet and legs surreptitiously moved out of sight behind them the clinking canisters of coins collected as gratuity for their performances.

This dance completed, they were able to continue answers to Lieutenant Watson's questions. "No we don't know where he is now," they smiled and shook their heads in unison, "haven't seen him here but he may be at the corner of Clark Street. He plays there sometimes."

Lieutenant Watson gave them a quick whisper of thanks and headed half way around the field along Clark Street. He saw no one on the corner but further along on Waveland he spotted a violin player. His spirits lifted as he approached the man.

"Seymour?" he asked as he came up to the man and interrupted his playing of whatever it was as it was unrecognizable.

The violinist stepped back and his eyes bulged with fear as he looked at Lieutenant Watson. He was so stunned he could not speak so Lieutenant Watson asked again, "Are you Seymour?"

The man shook his head first and then answered in a quivering voice, "I'm not Seymour."

"You are not Seymour?"

"I'm not Seymour."

The inquiry went along in this fashion with the answers the same as the questions.

Then it was, "Do you know him?"

"I don't know him."

"But he plays here - the violin."

"He plays here - the violin?"

"And you don't know him?"

"I don't know him."

The violinist was trembling now at being questioned so sternly by law enforcement. Yet he had a little quirk of bravado in him as he said under his breath, "We're legal, you know," and immediately took another step back away from Lieutenant Watson.

Lieutenant Watson said no more but shook his head as he walked away. He circled another block and came across a duo of jazzy banjo players. No trepidation here as they heartily greeted Lieutenant Watson.

"Glad to see you, glad to see you," they said as they shook his hand.

Lieutenant Watson reciprocated their "good friend" attitude and continued thus as he said he liked banjo music, that good old down home stuff; but now, alas, he was looking for a violin player.

The duo laughed as if the statement was outrageous.

"Really?" one said and poked his friend with an elbow. "Imagine that."

When Lieutenant Watson said, "Seymour" their voices joined together. "Seymour? Sure we know him, see him here often."

Lieutenant Watson was heartened by their exuberance. "He evidently is not around here today," he said. "I just would like to talk to him."

"Sure, sure," each one said.

Lieutenant Watson continued. "Can you tell me where he might be? Where he lives?"

Ah, the civilian dedication once again, thought Lieutenant Watson, as he unexpectedly received a precise answer. The banjo players knew that Seymour lived in an apartment building and the address was given. Now Lieutenant Watson had the information he wanted. He called for another car with two officers to follow him to the address on the west side to pick up a possible suspect in the Wrigley Field murder.

Lola, the tom cat, night prowler of the back alley and rat killer extraordinaire, met the force as he lay on the porch of the apartment building. He did not move until the building manager appeared at the door with a broom and hollered, "Get!" as he pricked Lola with the sharp wicks of the sweeper. Lola responded with a loud hiss, showing his dagger weapons of perfect incisors as he leaped from the porch.

Nodding approval of the building manager's actions, Lieutenant Watson identified himself and the two officers and then stated their mission.

"We're looking for a musician, a violin player exactly named Seymour. We are told he lives here".

The building manager became most cooperative.

"Yes, yes," he answered immediately. "Seymour, yes, he does live here, upstairs in the front apartment on the second floor."

"We want to talk to him," Lieutenant Watson stated.

The building manager obliginly stepped aside and pushed the broom behind him.

"Go right up," he said, "Yes, yes."

In the front apartment on the second floor stood Seymour, looking down on the happenings below. He was attracted to the window by the noise of the police arrival, their cars screeching back and forth as they crowded into the narrow street and then the formidable presence of the three policemen as they emerged and advanced on the building. He heard the building managers rebuke to Lola and the conversation that followed with a harsh sounding police man.

When he heard his name and that they were coming after him, Seymour stiffened and fear came upon him. They knew! They knew about his violin case!

Panic was added to his fear and he knew he had to flee, he had to get away. Without hesitation, he grabbed his violin case and ran out of the apartment into the hallway and headed for the back stairs.

Lieutenant Watson and the two officers were at the landing before the second floor. They saw Seymour running and Lieutenant Watson shouted, "He's going out the back way!"

This caused a scramble as one officer went down and out of the first floor to cover the back. Lieutenant Watson and the other officer continued up the stairs and down the hallway after Seymour.

Seymour was off to a good start as he jumped a few of the bottom stairs to reach the alley. Here he knew the jagged turns of the alley and the short cuts through yards without fences or gates. But out of his immediate neighborhood, he became unsure, still running but not aware of the direction he was going. He began to breathe faster and persperation was covering his face and he felt it was seeping along his body now. The sun was very hot and his violin case seemed heavier and he stumbled several times running through an open and overgrown area.

He was weary, he had little stamina for marathon running, but he saw a chance as an express way loomed ahead of him. On the other side was a quiet area of small houses built close together as a sub division. If he could get there, he could slow down and perhaps find a hiding place.

He stood at the side of the express way, studying the traffic in both directions. He could not move yet but he knew the policemen were getting close and he heard them shouting at him. Seymour made his plan as he saw the traffic on the other side was clear and on his side were only two cars and semi-truck just coming around the curve. He waited and then the two cars were passed and he made his run. Evidently, the two cars were slower than he thought and the semi-truck had accelerated on the curve for Seymour was trapped. He made a desparate jump and perhaps, for the first time in his life, his timing was off. The semi-truck hit him and sent him flying to the side of the road where he landed with a crunch, his violin case beside him,

Lieutenant Watson and the two officers reached him in the next instant but they could only look with dismay at the body and the life gone out of it. Lieutenant Watson took the violin case from Seymour's hand and opened it. They saw the blood on the instrument and beside it a bloody small Louisville Slugger bat and beside that a folded pack of money, it, too, stained with blood.

Seymour was identified as the killer of the camera man, the bloody bat was confirmed as the weapon, and the motive was robbery. The violin case, with all, was retained as evidence. The building manager of the apartment building quickly put Seymour's belongings, very little he was glad, and he gave it to charity. The street musicians came forward, almost as if hat in hand, and asked if... "whatever was"…they could give Seymour a decent burial. The TV station presented an admirable documentary on the camera man, extolling his virtues as a person and as a professional man of the camera.

And so the case was closed.

About three weeks later, another window in a room on the second floor of the apartment building was opened as wide as possible. The window was at the back of the building and was pushed to it's limits by Uncle Uno. He was a musician and was gone for the time in Wisconsin and Michigan playing a carnival and several fairs and outdoor events there. Uncle Uno played two instruments, flute and concertina, but was not a part of any performance. He played on the .periphery of events, holding forth as a soloist and accepting any contributions in the tin cannister at his feet.

The crowds at the carnivals and fairs were usually very friendly, eager to enjoy themselves, and out for a good time and so were glad to give to non-descript little man playing a flute or concertina and who smiled constantly in return for their generosity. Uncle Uno picked up quite a bit of change during the time he was there.

Eventually, he had to return home and the weather had been very hot while he was gone and, thus, he opened the window, fanned himself with his hands to help rid the stifling heated air from his place.

Uncle Uno was not his real name, of course, he was given that, with a little jest, when he held first chair as first flutist with the symphony orchestra. Then it all fell apart when a young, jealous wannabe reported the theft of the orchestras petty cash fund. He named Uncle Uno and he named correctly. Uncle Uno had taken it in a desparate situation and had every intention of paying it back but he was caught before that could happen. He was not pardoned but dismissed promptly from the orchestra. He returned to the symphony hall to try to plead his case, but was told he was disrupting rehearsals, escorted out, the door locked, and Uncle Uno stood alone on the pavement. He felt he was discredited and he could not join any other musical group with accusing eyes always looking at him.

Uncle Uno knew that his apartment would not cool quickly so he went out and down to the street to the diner where he had coffee and two doughnuts. When he left there, he stopped at the deli to pick up some food, being gone three weeks he had to replenish the larder. He selected a loaf of bread, a package of luncheon meat, and a quart of milk. He passed the fresh produce counter, happy that he had purchased and brought home several fresh, ripe Michigan peaches. He thought about the instant coffee, he had forgotten to check if there was a left. Better to get another, he thought, so he picked that up also.

When Uncle Uno returned to the apartment building, he was met by the building manager who stood on the porch waving a broom as if he were sweeping the entrance. The building manager heard Uncle Uno when he opened his window and when he made his way down the stairs and out of the building and he made his plan to meet Uncle Uno on his return. He scowled when he saw Lola lying against the bottom step on the sidewalk and who greeted Uncle Uno with a friendly flip of his tail and now cast a watchful eye on the building manager's broom.

The building manager greeted Uncle Uno with an insincere upturn of his lips which was not a smile. He was, in fact, not happy to see Uncle

Uno as he resented him as a musician who made his life and his job a headache. With Seymour gone, he had enjoyed peace and quiet for three weeks and now he had to contend with this one.

"You have been gone?" he said with a taunt "Vacation?"

Uncle Uno responded slowly, "I've been in Wisconsin and Michigan," then he added. "Working."

The building manager grimaced at the retort. Working, he thought, that only meant making that awful noise he called music. How often it riled him when he heard Uncle Uno and Seymour tooting and screeching on their instruments but his animosity came to the worst when the two of them got together to play La Paloma. They were on the front porch, of all places, and the horrible sounds scared people off the sidewalk and windows throughout the building were being closed, one after another. Even Lola was not entertained, he raised his head, his ears laid back on his head. He gave them a green eyed glare, hissed loudly, and ran off. Unfortunately, La Paloma, the dove, did not bring peace at that time.

The next morning after, the building manager feared for his job as an endless round or complaints descended on his door. Not only could he hear the raving comments, he could read the notes and papers tacked to his door which protested the "smelleroo flutino" and the "fertilizing fiddler" living within their boundaries.

Things quieted down in time, however, when the building manager informed Seymour and Uncle Uno, "No more. This is a zone of quiet, like a hospital".

"You haven't heard then about your friend?" he slyly asked Uncle Uno and noting the perplexed look on Uncle Uno's face, explained, "Seymour?"

"Seymour?" repeated Uncle Uno, remaining perplexed.

"He died," the building manager replied, trying not to sound too grateful.

Now Uncle Uno responded with a complete surprised expression. His eyes opened wide and stared with disbelief, his words almost inaudible. "Seymour... dead?"

"About three weeks ago," the building manager continued, glad to have surprised and disturbed Uncle Uno.

"Three weeks ago, you say?" Uncle Uno asked.

"Yes, yes," the building manager answered swiftly, "after he killed and robbed a man at Wrigley Field."

Uncle Uno now was stunned and he could only whisper, "Seymour did that?"

"The police came for him," the building manager went on and then added, "police were swarming all over the place." He was in control, he thought, and a little exaggeration would not hurt. "Nothing like that happened around here before." He conveyed that it added disrespect for the lodgings. "The police chased Seymour right out of here; he got over to the expressway and got hit by a truck."

Uncle Uno was a stunned audience and he began to tremble. "Three weeks ago?" he stammered.

"Yes, yes," the building manager said with impatience," on the 5th of the month. I know because it was the day his rent was up, like justice."

This statement so shocked Uncle Uno further and his trembling increased so that he dropped his bag of groceries and it landed on Lola. Lola screamed and leaped and landed up on the porch next to the broom. The building Manager swing the broom but Lola screamed again, leaped over the broom, and landed on the building manager's feet. Now the building manager screamed and tried to kick Lola but the broom was stiff in front of him, sent him backwards as he stumbled and fell against the railing.

Drat cat! the building manager thought, always hanging around. He suspected Lola belonged to one of the tenants but it was always denied and he could never track the movements of the wily cat so he did not know. Now that he had pronounced justice upon Seymour, he vowed that from now on all leases would state no instruments and no pets!

Uncle Uno was in such a state that he gave no response to the slap stick performance of Lola and the building manager. His movements were mechanical. He picked up his bag of groceries, passed the performers, and entered the building. On the second floor at the top of the stairs, he stopped and looked at Seymour's door. He was no longer there, he was gone, and it was silent. Uncle Uno walked slowly down the hallway to his own door, to his own apartment. The room was still quite warm but it was not oppresive. He checked his bag of groceries, the jar of instant coffee was not broken so apparently it had landed on Lola's tail.

He might turn on the fan now but he was not sure. He could not make up his mind what to do. His thoughts were on Seymour and he was imagining all that he had been told: Seymour killing and robbing a man, running and being chased by police, then hit by a truck. He tried to see it again, he tried to imagine it again, but he could not bring it to reality.

On this same day, another native returned. Detective Daniel Rankin, head of the Homicide Division, came back to the precinct. He had been on official leave of absence for about a month, attending a conference on Homeland Security which included a tour of several cities to study the latest readiness plans. He was an observer of mock survival exercises with fake bombs blasts and responses of healthy looking individuals acting as victims, wrapped in gauze, staggering and lifted about, rescued and treated in a real war games fashion.

After these exercises, Detective Rankin decided to take time and travel to many communities, around and about, to present his program on Neighborhood Crime Watchers. A bit more mundane, perhaps, but he thought it important to caution the citizens to be alert and keep their lights on.

"Good morning, Scooter," he said with cheerfulness as he stepped into the department.

He received an equally cheerful greeting from Scooter. "Good morning, sir," spoken with joy and then a wide smile.

"Come into my office, Scooter," Detective Rankin said with a nod, "whenever you are ready and up date me on the happenings while I was gone."

Knowing that Detective Rankin was returning, Scooter had the "up date" already prepared and was in the office before Detective Rankin had hardly settled in.

"Lieutenant Watson did very well," Scooter began and then gave the details: "three murders, one being the Seymour case at Wrigley Field; two drive by shootings; four robberies, three banks and one cab driver; a child had disappeared; a university student mysteriously poisoned; and a drowning in the lake."

How good to be home, Detective Rankin thought as he relaxed in his chair behind his deak.

He nodded his approval of the report and then asked, "Any new developments on the grocery store case?"

"No, sir," Scooter answered.

"Thank you, Scooter," Detective Rankin said, "Good job, well done."

"Glad you are back, sir," Scooter added hurriedly as he stepped out of the office.

The grocery store case questioned by Detective Rankin was the last case he was working on before his leave. A grocery store owned by a Vietnamese was robbed by three masked gunmen and the owner was killed. Detective Rankin decided to review his notes on the case and, fortunately, the store had a surveillance tape of the happening. Detective Rankin decided to rerun the tape. It showed the three men entering the store with weapons drawn. The Vietnamese was a fiesty little man and his response was to pull out a shot gun from behind the counter and start blasting away. Fire power erupted all over and Detective Rankin thought it was like the "O K Corral". Counters and shelves exploded; the mustard connected to the ketchup, the ketchup connected to the mayo, the mayo connected to the salad dressing, the French, the Ranch, and the Cucumber. When it was over, the gunmen fled, the owner was dead, and only one of the robbers was caught, trapped, and slain by the Homicide Department led by Detective Rankin.

Detective Rankin just had rewound the tape when there was a knock on the door then Scooter stepped into the office.

"Sir, a man is here to see you," he began, "Said his name is Uncle Uno."

Detective Rankin gave him a puzzled look. "Did you say"...(pause)... "Uncle Uno?"

'That's what he said," Scooter replied, "and it is about the Seymour case."

The puzzled look remained on Detective Rankin's face.

Scooter recognized that his "up date" report had not included sufficient details so he quickly explained. "The murder at Wrigley Field. Seymour robbed and killed a TV camera man. Lieutenant Watson traced him down and went to arrest him; but Seymour ran taking the evidence, his violin case, with him. Seymour tried to cross the expressway but was hit and killed. The officers got the violin case, opened it to see not only the violin but the bat. . ."

"The bat?" interrupted Detective Rankin, more puzzled than ever.

"Miniature, sir, given away at the game," Scooter went on. "It was covered with blood and the money was there too. It is now in the lab file."

Detective Rankin nodded but had no more to say than, "Well, show the man in, Scooter." But he thought what more could be said to that.

Detective Rankin rose from behind his desk and went forward to meet the timid looking little man who had just entered his office.

"Uncle Uno?" he asked quickly after which he received a whispered, "Yes." So he held out his hand for a shake and felt the hand trembling. "I'm Detective Rankin," he went on, speaking in a quiet tone.

Uncle Uno was obviously frightened and nervous to be in these surroundings as he did not move from the doorway and his wide eyed look went back and forth around the room.

"Have a seat," Detective Rankin said, still holding the hand as he led Uncle Uno to a chair in front of his desk. Detective Rankin returned to his place behind the desk, careful not to scrutinize Uncle Uno too closely and upset him even more.

A moment passed before Uncle Uno seemed to relax and then speak.

"I want to tell you about Seymour," he said.

Detective Rankin nodded, preparing to be a listener as was his custom, knowing through experience that he learned much when people went on and told their own story.

"They said Seymour killed a man," Uncle Uno stated.

Detective Rankin nodded.

"At Wrigley Field," Uncle Uno went on, speaking a little easier.

Detective Rankin nodded.

"But Seymour did not do it," Uncle Uno continued, "because he was with me."

Now Detective Rankin did not nod. He steadied his face and looked directly at Uncle Uno "What do you mean, he was with you?"

"Well, you see, we are musicians, Seymour and I. Not for hire, of course, but we go on our own and when something is going on, we stand aside and play," He paused. "I play two instruments, flute and concertina, and Seymour plays violin. People give us change if they care to."

Detective Rankin wondered if his question had rattled Uncle Uno and made him confused; although he knew about these wandering musicians, one instrument or two or whatever, but they were not a troublesome group as a whole, However, he did not want Uncle Uno to avoid his question.

"So you and Seymour were playing to get change?" he asked.

"We were in Wisconsin," Uncle Uno repled, "there was a carnival outside of Milwaukee and Seymour and I were there. Then I went to Madison, a few fairs were going on around there and I headed toward Appleton for the circus and then I went over to Michigan for a show."

Wandering musicians indeed, thought Detective Rankin. "Just a minute, Uncle Uno," he said as it sounded like a lot of nervous ranting and he wanted clarification. "You mean you and Seymour were all over Wisconsin and Michigan?"

"Oh, no," Uncle Uno answered quickly, "not Seymour, only me. Seymour was with me only that one day at the carnival. He wanted to get back and go into Indiana because there were possibilities there. The carnival closed that day and at midnight Seymour took a bus and came home."

Now Detective Rankin got the understanding that, in this weird scenario, Uncle Uno was asserting that Seymour was with him in Wisconsin for one day only.

Detective Rankin stated this observation. "So you and Seymour were in Wisconsin for one day only?"

Now Uncle Uno nodded. "The day of the murder."

"So you and Seymour played one day, that day, at the carnival?" he asked for definition.

"Oh, no," Uncle Uno hurriedly said again. "Seymour was with me but he did not play. He left his violin at home because he was planning on going to Indiana, like I said."

Detective Rankin was quiet for the moment, then asked thoughtfully as he had to be certain. "So Seymour did not take his violin in it's case when he went with you to Wisconsin?"

Uncle Uno nodded.

"And he was there until midnight?" Detective Rankin continued.

"That's what I mean; that's what I want you to know; he was with me."

Uncle Uno answered and the nervousness returned as his voice was shaky.

Detective Rankin now was fully aware of the implications of Uncle Uno's story, but his countenance could not reflect the gravity he felt. Instead, he gave Uncle Uno a slight smile.

"I thank you for coming," he said as he rose and came around to shake Uncle Uno's hand again. He walked him to the door but there they stopped as Uncle Uno turned to Detective Rankin and said, "I just didn't want Seymour remembered as a murderer."

To this, Detective Rankin could only nod his head.

After Uncle Uno left, Detective Rankin asked Scooter to come into his office. He began to relate Uncle Uno's story and he watched the gamut of surprised expressions that came over Scooter's face. First, his eyes widen and then amazement settled on his countenance and made his eyes grow even wider. The gaze was fixed for a while then changed as he squinted and a scowl of disbelief creased his forehead. At the last, his jaws dropped open and a resounding "No!" came forth from his mouth as his lips pursed the word and followed with "Not true."

"Unfortunately," Detective Rankin responded, "it was what he told me."

The completely puzzled Scooter answered quickly, "It was obvious; the case was closed and the evidence was in."

"I am aware of that," Detective Rankin replied slowly.

Scooter looked closely at Detective Rankin, trying to study his response and then had to ask, " do you believe him?"

Detective Rankin did not answer immediately to allow the question to assume an importance.

"All we have to do," he said at last "is to disprove this Uncle Uno's story."

He rose from his desk and went towards a large cabinet across the room. "I will go over the file, just for certainty," he paused to speak as casually as possible. "If Lieutenant Watson is in, Scooter, would you have him come to see me?"

A still puzzled Scooter left and Detective Rankin got out the file on the Seymour case. He carefully studied Lieutenant Watson 's report and then surveyed the gruesome photographs of the crime: the smashed skull of the camera man, that violin case, both closed and open to reveal the smudged instrument, a wad of money, and that small bat drenched with blood.

Scooter evidently followed his instructions with alacrity for soon he was back at the office door to inform Detective Rankin that Lieutenant Watson had just returned to the department from detail. Just as he finished the announcement, he stepped aside as Lieutenant Watson appeared.

"Come in, both of you Detective Rankin invited. It was for a reason, an important one for him. The Seymour case had to be reviewed and that was a difficult task and one which he disliked considerably. He had to bring it up with the officer who had solved and closed a case and he did not want to imply incompetence. It could rankle feelings deeply and Detective Rankin had little satisfaction in doing so.

So it was now with Lieutenant Watson. Detective Rankin knew Lieutenant Watson was a good officer, diligent and capable. In fact, Detective Rankin himself had recommended Lieutenant Watson to be in charge of his department while he was on recent leave. Yet, he knew Lieutenant Watson was a bit too sensitive to criticism, he became easily defensive and responded at times in short temper. That was why Detective Rankin requested Scooter to be there because three in attendance would be more apt to take any edge off which could be more likely in a one on one confrontation.

Once again, Detective Rankin told Uncle Uno's story and Lieutenant Watson's reaction was much like that of Scooter: surprise and shock but with a pronounced dimension of anger.

"Not another musician!" was the outburst of Lieutenant Watson. "You believe such a story?"

Detective Rankin did not reply immediately which distressed Lieutenant Watson the more.

"That Seymour was guilty," he ranted on, "guilty as could be. He ran, tried to get away and took the evidence with him. The weapon, the bat, was right there!" He looked quickly at Scooter who nodded in agreement.

It was what Detective Rankin hoped for; an assurance for Lieutenant Watson.

"I know, I know," Detective Rankin answered calmly.

But Lieutenant Watson went on. "Well, this Uncle somebody, a musician he says, is lying, He is covering up for one of his own kind."

"I know, Lieutenant," Detective Rankin repeated, still calm. "You did a fine job and your report..." he paused to nod to Scooter... "is well documented." He paused once more to allow for release of any tensions. "But we have an obligation to check this Uncle Uno's story."

Another pause took place and Detective Rankin felt the slight easing of tension and he could tell Lieutenant Watson what he had told Scooter. "We have to check this story until we can disprove it."

"And how are you to do that?" was the retort from Lieuteant Watson.

A good question, thought Detective Rankin, and he appeared puzzled. Then he smiled slightly and answered, "Well, we can find out if the batter was left handed or right handed."

Lieutenant Watson stared in disbelief and Scooter snickered but quickly covered his mouth as of to suppress a cough.

No more was spoken but Lieutenant Watson threw up his hands in disgust walked out.

Detective Rankin pretended no notice of Scooter's snicker and cough, although he was not displeased and proceeded in a light hearted manner.

"We will really begin," he said, "by checking the dates and places of all carnivals, fairs, and other such attractions in Wisconsin and Michigan. Can you get on that right away, Scooter? The tourist bureaus will help."

Scooter nodded and subdued any additional joviality

"Oh, and while you are at it," Detective Rankin went on, "check out Indiana as well," as he remembered that Seymour was interested in "possibilities" there.

Sensing a serious and getting down to business attitude, Scooter now became his professional self and hurried toward the door and out to his desk to undertake the instructions given.

Detective Rankin stopped him immediately. "Scooter, there was one eye witness in this case: the fan who sat in the upper grandstand. Call him, please, and ask him to come in; just for a talk."

In another minute, Detective Rankin passed Scooter at his desk and announced, "I'm going out to the TV station where the camera man worked and I'll talk to them."

Detective Rankin was greeted with cordiality at the TV station. He was known to them just as he knew them. However, when a homicide detective walks in it was certain to arouse curiosity along with the friendly greeting. These TV people had a sharp instinct for a story so anticipation could be mixed in as well. All eyes looked at him in wonder when he announced that he wanted to see the film the deceased camera man made on the Seymour case at Wrigley Field.

Detective Rankin explained that he had been away on leave at the time and was only doing a professional duty to review the case. He tried to express this with no unusual concern.

Now the reporter who had accompanied the camera man on this mission came forward, was glad to oblige the detective, smiled with a hint of suspicion, but did not ask for a reason.

Taking charge, the reporter secured the film and was leading Detective Rankin to the screening room. Along the way and being astute as to possible questions, the reporter began to relate his opinion of the camera man. A friend, he said, worked together for a long time, always professional, had no enemies or created any trouble. He was missed by all.

This, of course, was exactly what Detective Rankin would have asked and he sensed that the reporter knew this.

The film began and the first picture was of Wrigley Field, taken toward the outfield showing the bleachers under the large scoreboard and the vines which were thick along the wall. Detective Rankin smiled at the scene so familar to him.

The focus next was on the reporter with an interview of a young pitcher called up from the farm system. He had pitched fairly well the previous day but did not win the game. The pitcher admitted his lack of major league experience but was eager and determined to learn and grateful for his chance to be in big time.

Then the reporter came on and announced the starting pitchers for the day's game giving their won and lost records and how they had done against each other. The reporter concluded that the home team was hoping to play five hundred ball.

That was it, nothing unusual or questionable there, nothing to pick upon for the murder investigation.

As Detective Rankin was leaving, he was aware once again of the eyes upon him from the office staff but now he could sense the whispers also. Why was he here? What is he looking for? But Detective Rankin only smiled and thanked the reporter.

Yet, the reporter asked, "Anything new, detective?"

Detective Rankin shook his head but the reporter went on.

"Let us know," he said and smiled back at Detective Rankin, "if we can be of help."

When Detective Rankin left the TV station, he decided to go to the apartment building where Seymour had lived to see if anything there could be of interest or importance. He arrived there to find a lazy looking cat stretched out on the porch and washing his face and limbs. Detective Rankin had to step over him as the cat did not move or look at him and just continued his toilet. However, when Detective Rankin met the building manager, identified himself, and explained his mission to talk to the tenants, he was met with extreme consternation.

The building manager had to agree, of course, but his mind was teeming with discouraging thoughts. Another police man around here, the thoughts went. What now? Do I have to begin giving back ground checks to everyone and I have already forbidden instruments and pets, but he had to give a quiet "yes" to Detective Rankin's request.

Detective Rankin's quest, however, provided little information or clues as the residents reflected the notion that there was safety in not interfering. Didn't bother me…didn't see anyone…nothing suspicious…

didn't bother me, it went. There was little communication with Seymour, less caring, and no interest in his coming and going.

Not on the first level of the apartment building. When Detective Rankin ascended to the second floor, he heard the faint sound of music, a slight scale of tones, coming from the far end of the corridor; and he knew it must be from Uncle Uno's apartment. He need not go there, he knew, but the consensus of information he received at other doors was much the same as he had received before on the lower level.

Except for one elderly man. He lived in the apartment next to what had been Seymours.

"Yes, I saw him," the elderly man said.

"Tell me," Detective Rankin said quickly.

"Well, you see," the man hesitated and smiled sheepishly, "I have to get up several times at night you know…"

Detective Rankin nodded knowingly.

"Well, it was early in the morning and I heard someone at Seymour's door. I was up, you know…" another hesitation…"so I looked out my door but it was only Seymour. Unusual because Seymour never stayed out late like that."

Detective Rankin had to get this testimony straight so he repeated slowly to the old man. "You actually saw Seymour coming home early in the morning?"

The elderly man nodded, "Yes, I was up, you know…" He said as if in defence of his statement. "Then, later the police came and chased Seymour down this hallway; but I saw him early in the morning because I write down the time I…"

Detective Rankin nodded knowingly again. "One more thing," he asked, "when you saw Seymour early in the morning, did he have his violin case with him?"

"No, the elderly man answered, "I didn't see that."

When Detective Rankin descended the stairs to the first floor, he saw the building manager awaiting there, obviously peeved, and with a curious and questioning look upon his face.

Detective Rankin stopped before him and after the no-nothing, no-seeing reponses he got from most of the occupants, he said , "You know, I would recommend you get a surveillance camera for this building."

Surveillance camera! The look on the building manager's face changed immediately to that of dumbfounder as he stared after Detective Rankin.

When Detective Rankin returned to the department, he saw a skinny looking man seated in the vestibule. Scooter quickly introduced him as the man who was at the ball game at Wrigley Field. Detective Rankin, now aware of the identity, nodded knowingly in thanks to Scooter. With that, he shook the man's hand, thanked him for coming, and invited him into his office.

When the man stood up, he was tall as well as skinny and he wore a gray sweat shirt which had the word BIG on the front and BANG on the back when he turned around. Detective Rankin smiled to himself as he followed the man into his office. He bade the man sit down and now he smiled at him, face to face.

In a friendly manner, Detective Rankin began, "I understand you were at the game at Wrigley Field when the murder occurred?"

The man did not wait for further questions or explanations but began to talk.

"Man was it hot!" he stated "I almost took my shirt off!"

Detective Rankin wondered if the man realized he had inquired about murder, not the weather. Yet, he did not want to be harsh with the man at this point; so he said, still in a friendly tone, "I heard about that, the weather, I mean; but I was gone for several weeks and did not experience it." This was spoken to put forth, if the man could get the point, as a reason for being called in. "But the weather did not keep you from the game, did it? You were there?"

"For the whole game, would not leave," the man answered, speaking as if in conversation, not interrogation.

"You had good seats, I presume, in the upper deck?" Detective Rankin continued, not liking to have to give information rather than receive it.

"I like it there, up high, and look down at all the action. Really good, really good." The man smiled at that,

"And there was a lot of action that day, was there not?" Detective Rankin questioned, trying to steer the man toward the information that he wanted to hear.

"Oh, yeah," came the reply, "a really good game."

"But won by a home run in the ninth inning?" Well, thought Detective Rankin, if he had to press for the information, he would.

"Man, that ball was hit!" Out of the park and across the street! It was sailing!"

"You could easily see that?"

"You 're right, all that."

"Tell me about the murder," Detective Rankin asked and now he looked steadily at the man and did not smile. "You saw that?"

The man looked at Detective Rankin and noted his serious gaze.

"Well, I didn't see that," the man replied slowly. "I didn't know about that until I left the park and got down to the street. A real mess."

"Before that, while you were at the game in the upper deck, you reported," Detective Rankin paused. "I have read the official report, and that you saw someone walking around there, wearing a straw hat and carrying a violin case."

"Yes," the man answered, "I saw that."

"Can you tell me anything more about this person, identify him more clearly: clothing, the walk, shape, some thing odd or personal about him?"

The man was silent for a moment. He frowned at the question and then he laughed.

"Why are you asking me that? Man, I was too far above for that! Looking down! All I could see was the top of the straw hat and the violin case, nothing more. Man, I don't know!"

Detective Rankin stood up from his desk, knowing that the interview was over. He thanked the man and saw him to the door. He stood there and said to himself, "I wish I could say 'man, I don 't know, too'" He had to smile regardless as he saw BANG go out.

Standing in the doorway, he saw Scooter coming and carrying several sheets of paper in his hand.

Scooter looked after the departed also and approached Detective Rankin with a questionable look upon his face. "Did his shirt say BANG?"

Detective Rankin nodded but said, "Nothing new from there."

"Well," Scooter said, handing the sheets of paper to Detective Rankin, "here is the information from Wisconsin, Michigan, and Indiana on all outdoor attractions that took place in each state."

Detective Rankin thanked Scooter and took the papers to his desk where he studied them carefully, especially the dates of the attractions which were performed at the time of the murder at Wrigley Field. He noted immediately that the date of the carnival outside of Milwaukee closed on the same date as the murder. He checked other dates of fairs and circuses that Uncle Uno had mentioned in his wanderings around Wisconsin and they fit into his time frame. Uncle Uno had gone over to Michigan, he said, and there was an Art Show in Saugatuck at that time.

Then Detective Rankin turned to Indiana, starting at the Northwest corner. Seymour thought that might be the start of possibilities. Truly, they were a lively bunch over there. They had a Pierogi Fest that lasted several days. It included a picnic in a park with games and outdoor dancing.

Another close area had a Popcorn Fair that started with a parade of floats created by business and civic organizations and led by winners of a King and Queen Popcorn contest. Needless to state, the event ended with a grand display of fireworks.

After reading these listings, Detective Rankin sat silent for a moment and thought seriously about what he had read. It became evident to him that Uncle Uno's story could be documented. The date of the Wrigley Field murder was also the last day and night of the Wisconsin carnival. According-ing to Uncle Uno, Seymour was there that day and up to midnight when the carnival closed and returned home in the early hours of the following morning and seen by an elderly neighbor with an over active bladder. Most importantly to Detective Rankin was that these two old gents confirmed that Seymour did not have his violin case with him at this time.

There was one last thing that Detective Rankin wanted to do. He called the morgue to talk to his good friend Sam, the mortcian.

"Dan!" answered Sam in a. loud voice. "Glad to hear from you; you have been away!"

"On security planning and such issues," Detective Rankin replied easily. "Well worth the while, but happy to be back, getting into the routine again."

"That I can believe," Sam said and it was loud and, for a mortician, a surprising boisterous voice.

"Speaking of which, I have a favor to ask; I have a question," Detective Rankin paused for a moment and then continued, "which you might think is silly."

Sam laughed and that was boisterous also and echoed on the phone line. "Dan, you know me, no question has ever been silly."

"That murder that happened several weeks ago at Wrigley Field. Remember? The man got hit with a small bat."

Sam laughed again. "I remember, all right."

Now Detective Rankin tried to laugh, "Can you tell if the batter was left handed or right handed?"

"Always the baseball fan," Sam replied. "Well, from the place where the head was struck the hardest and the deepest, I would say the batter was left handed."

"Thank you, Sam."

Detective Rankin sat back in his chair and sighed as he tried to relax and let his thoughts forge slowly around and settle after the events and the exercises of his day. His foremost thought was of so much for disapproval. He had put forth that idea on Uncle Uno's testimony to Lieutenant Watson and Scooter and it had failed. With complete naiveti and sincerity, Uncle Uno had challenged the entire concept that Seymour was guilty of murder. Thus, his thoughts centered on Seymour and the puzzle of how all this came about.

Detective Rankin had known Seymour for many years and of his so called concerts in various places around and about. He thought Seymour a simple man, harmless, although he had in fact once arrested him. That was several years back when Daniel Rankin was a fledgling cop on the force. He was called to an altercation outside of the Nature Museum of the city. Seymour was playing there on a sunny afternoon when a live moth got loose in an unguarded moment from the exhibit. Not witnessing this insect's flight for freedom was a tourist lady in a sun dress printed with Tahitian flowers. Completely surprised when the moth landed with fluttering wings on her halter, she screamed and rushed out of the building and threw a moth into Seymour's violin case. Seymour had paused for a moment to refresh himself with a can of pop. He took this action by the lady as a personal assault to his beloved instrument and with an impulsive instinct to defend it, he threw the can of pop at her. The open can hit her on the forehead, scraping the skin and a trickle of blood gave her three eyebrows. The pop spilled out like a rainfall over her sun dress with Tahitian flowers.

Officer Rankin had to arrest Seymour and send the lady to the emergency room of a nearby hospital. Seymour had to be held until the lady emerged with a band aid (3/4 inch) on her forehead, a plumped up right eye, and the Tahitian flowers on her dress withered in brown colored pop just as real flowers when they fade.

In all that, the lady tried to be dignified and show some composure as, with a toss of her head, stated that she would not press charges against THAT MUSCIAN!

Officer Rankin remembered how frightened Seymour became by the event and actually shook with fear when he was arrested. When told the reason was assault, Seymour almost fell to the ground and Officer Rankin had to hold him up. Remorse filled him so deeply that he could not rejoice when told the charges were dropped and he was dismissed.

This picture now came back to Detective Rankin and he saw Seymour as he did then. No way could he see Seymour take a swing with a bat, even a small one, and crush a man's skull and rob him. However, he had to face the fact that a serious problem existed; it was a far cry from a moth to a bloody bat in Seymour's violin case. Yet, the image of a frightened Seymour would not go away. Instead, it went on to picture a terrified Seymour when he opened his case, saw what was there and heard the police coming for him. The only thing for him was to run.

Detective Rankin sighed again and now the most worrisome thought came to him. If not Seymour, then someone else had to do the killing. Someone who had stolen Seymour's violin case to be used in a miurder and then returned it to his apartment for Seymour to be blamed.

Someone else...and that Detective Rankin was to know when the Milwaukee Brewers were coming to Wrigley Field for a three game series with the Cubs.

"Darling, we are going to the game tonight."

Ah, the voice that gave another reason for Detective Rankin to be glad to be home. Perhaps two reasons: going to the baseball game and being with Ulla. It might be stated in another way: being home with Ulla and going to the baseball game. Both, however, were affairs of the heart.

When he stepped through the doorway into the living room, he sensed her presence there. Not only the soft voiced greeting but the small and caring things she did for him. The light was on over the closet door which was opened for the place of his own where he always removed his police man's trappings of hat and jacket, suits, badge and weapons.

Another light came from the kitchen which carried her quick movements around stove, refrigerator, and table as she set forth a feast of good cooking for him. From there also came the one sweet aroma of cardamom from baked rolls she had prepared especially for what she called his home coming. Following these delights to the kitchen, the best of all was she alone with a radiant smile turned toward him and the pleasure of a kiss.

It was the same feeling he had experienced when he first met Ulla. He had been on the force for a few years when he was assigned as part of local, security protection for a Swedish tennis star coming to commemorate Scandinavian Day. The event was held out doors at a local park for a day. The security detail was entitled to meals. Daniel Rankin was scheduled for lunch and he made his way to a pavilion set up for food services. The menu was listed on a large poster at the side of the counter. He was studying the poster when he heard someone ask:

"May I help you?"

He turned to look upon the prettiest face he had ever seen, framed in pale yellow blonde hair and deep blue eyes and she smiled with those eyes too.

"Pancakes," Daniel Rankin said, not knowingly, but the last thing he had seen on the menu poster.

"Lingon?"

Still in a trance like state, he wondered: what did she say? Did she speak in a foreign language?

She laughed with amusement and then said, "Lingon berries. On the pancakes."

"Oh, yes," he answered quickly though he had never heard of such a thing but he probably would have said yes to anything she asked.

That is how he met Ulla Jacobson. Daniel Rankin was smitten; he was a goner.

With his detective skills...ahem…he found out that she was a cashier at a known restaurant and that is where he went when he wanted to see her again.

He sat at a table where he could gaze upon her. Her position as a cashier was at a counter near the window of the restaurant. The light from outside reflected on her hair and made it brighter, almost like a halo.

When he approached her to pay his check, he had used several coins for the payment. Unfortunately, but fortunately for him, her hand was small and the coins started to spill over. Quickly, he reached out and caught her hand and held it while she counted out the money. Her hand was soft and warm in his and she kept it there while slowly shifting and adding the coins. When she finished, she smiled at him and said, "It was just right."

Afterwards, Daniel Rankin came to eat a lot of pancakes, lingon berries or not, and, on purpose, he paid his checks with a lot of small change. Could this be classified as courtship? Or what?

Nevertheless, whatever it is called, it took a positive turn when Daniel took Ulla, upon her request, to a service called Luciafest at her church. Not wanting to place anyone in a state of perturbation by this service, a brief explanation should be forthcoming. It is a day, December 13, when the northern people are faced with the shortest daylight, or the longest darkness, of the year. To this, the Swedes began the service of light named after Saint Lucia by having the oldest daughter of a household wear a crown of lighted candles on her head and expressing a joy by serving coffee and pastry to all members of the household.

Ulla wanted to attend the service at her chuch because she had been a Lucia Queen in her early teens. In proof, she showed a photograph of this time in her early life to Daniel. She was as beautiful then as she was now, Daniel thought, as he looked at her rounded cheeks, smiling lips, steady blue eyes and longer blonde hair that fell around the shoulders of her white robe. But he was struck by the burning candles set in the crown on her head. It seemed to him that the candle light flickered in the picture and cast a halo around her. Another halo! To him, a favorable sign and he proposed. So Daniel Rankin and Ulla Jacobson were married in her Lutheran Church and it can be said again: "It was just right."

The homecoming celebration was going along fine with the evening at the baseball game. Dan and Ulla had good seats along the third base line. It had been a hot day, but with the sun settled down, the setting was cooler and occasionally a cool breeze from the lake would float across Wrigley Field.

A young rookie pitcher was starting for the Milwaukee Brewers. He had beaten the Cubs once before and now was taking the mound for a second try. The Cubs were going with a veteran pitcher who had experienced arm trouble but were anxious and hopeful to return him to a regular spot in the rotation.

Dan settled back to enjoy the game. He felt overly contented and satisfied after the gala dinner Ulla had prepared. To this he felt the glow within from the feeling of being happy where you are. This feeling began from the first time his father brought him to Wrigley Field and never did it diminish. Always there was the excitement and enthusiasm of the ball game.

This dedication increased at a time when he wanted to go back further and wonder about what happened at the beginning. He went to the archives and, as many times happens, getting to the roots can be quite surprising.

The biggest surprise was that this place was indeed hallowed ground. The site at Addison Street near Sheffield Avenue started as a seminary in October of 1891 when a mission chapel of the Lutheran Church was established there. Hallowed ground expanded in 1893 when a first seminary building was built as the president's residence at Sheffield and Waveland. A second building next to it became known as Eliza Hall, named after the wife of the first president of the Board of Directors and had four class rooms, a library, and the student dormitory.

This was becoming serious religious outreach as the seminary officially opened in 1896 at St. Mark's Lutheran Church on the original site at Addison and Sheffield. In 1910 this property was sold and the seminary moved to Maywood.

So this clump of land was to be church on this part of the North Side, but what happened? Four years later, in 1914, a man named Charles H. Weeghman purchased property at Clark and Addison and constructed, what else, but Weeghman Park with a seating capacity of 14,000 for his Federal League team, The Whales. Unfortunate move for the Federal League folded after the 1915 season. Then what did Weeghman do? He purchased the Chicago Cubs and moved them to Weeghmau Park.

Now the speculation. What happened between 1910 when the Lutherans left and 1914 when Weeghman showed up? Dan thought he had it figured out: the Lutherans screwed up. Did the spirit go out? Was there more a squabble between church and state? Or was there more promising land elsewhere? Whatever, the ground was desolate. Weeghman came in and tried to get something going: building a park, bringing in a team, but no joy prevailed and the failures began; and he brought the Cubs into all this mess.

Dan figured it out, he thought, but kept his ideas all to himself, especially for Ulla. She was the dearest person in all the world to him so how could he even hint to her that he thought the curse of the Cubs was the Lutherans. Think of Weeghman's team, the Whales. Perhaps they sank with the Federal League but their name changed to The Wails and could be heard through out the ages.

The wailing began in the sixth inning. The pitching had been good, the young pitcher for the Brewers and the veteran for the Cubs had locked in a battle that kept either team from scoring. It had gone thus into the Cubs sixth that the game reached a turning point. The veteran started well, getting two outs, but then he began to lose his edge as he walked two batters. He seemed to struggle as he gave out wide and off the plate pitches; his early effectiveness was missing. A pause was made and after a mound conference with the coaches, the pitcher was removed with a strained muscle in his right side. This condition was detected earlier and had remained a concern. Relief came from the bull pen but did not obtain the final out before one run was scored for the Brewers.

Hopes rising, the Brewers scored twice more in the seventh inning and the Cubs used three relief pitchers before the inning was over but the Brewers were leading 3 to 0.

Not surrendering, the Cubs struck back and scored two rums in the eighth. The lead off hitter started the inning with a double. Wailing ceased for a while but not it's undercurrent as the next batter hit an easy infield out and could not move the runner to third. The next hitter, however, got another double and scored the first. A following single hit brought the other man home from second and he made it because he was a fast runner. The Cubs were challenging now with two runs and the hope was to hold the Brewers and get at least a tie in the ninth inning.

The Brewers did not think so, however, as in the ninth, the young pitcher was replaced with a pinch hitter and he came forward with a triple, scored on a fly out and upped the score to 4 to 2. One run may have seemed possible for the Cubs but two were harder to come by and the Cubs could not score either way and the big letter L came up on the scoreboard and the wailing goes on.

Dan and Ulla rose stretched thenselves, but waited by their seats for a right moment to move into the crowd of fans as they were leaving. They did not move, however, as Dan saw a security guard coming toward them and there was an anxious look upon his face.

"Detective Rankin," he said, "can you come up to the Press Box? Something happened."

Dan nodded and took Ulla's hand as they followed the security guard. They ran a maze like walk as they made their way through the slowly departing fans and it took a bit longer to trek the many stairs up to the high level of the Press Box. Several more security guards were there and Dan acknowledged them as he passed them in the corridor. There he left Ulla, telling her to stay with the guards as he entered into the Press Box. He stopped instantly as he saw before him the sports writer, T.O.D. Poole, slumped over the shelf with his head bowed before his computer screen and a rope encircled around his neck.

Dan immediately gave directions to the guards: call homicide unit, request the crime lab appear quickly, and do not move or touch anything. These orders were dispatched without delay and almost as quickly executed. The homicide and the crime lab units were instructed to enter Wrigley Field through the security doors so as to avoid or attract attention from the still crowded streets around the park.

Dan's critical and experienced eye for detail looked again at the scene before him. It looked anything but shocking. T.O.D. Poole's body could have fallen forward in a swoon, half face down. His head lay on a tablet of papers that probably were his notes and report of the game. Aside to that was a set of well sharpened pencils. The computer screen had gone blank and quiet as if in obeisance to the bowed head. The visible half of T.O.D. Poole was without bruise or blemish. At the end of the table shelf was an unopened carton from Food Service. No struggle or messy movements of any sort were evident. Yet, all this was gone and perverted by that tight rope around T.O.D. Poole's neck. It was murder by strangulation and if that could be acceptable in any way, it would be that the killing was quick and easy.

Dan stepped out of the Press Box and went to put his arm around Ulla's shoulders.

"T.O.D. is dead," he said softly to her.

She gasped and a frightened look came upon her face.

"The crime lab workers are here," he went on, "and we will know more later." He did not want to use the words murder or strangulation to her, but only the thought that an explanation of it all would be forthcoming. To Dan, however, other thoughts were more troublesome.. He sensed that the murder of T.O.D. Poole was planned and carried out and related, somehow, to the murder of the camera man with Wrigley Field used as the stage and why that? What purpose? A frightening scenario was in the making.

With his arm still around Ulla, Dan pulled themselves away as the now busy and earnest work was being done by the lab technicians. Dan and Ulla did not get far when they were met and stopped by a security guard leading a shaky and confused youth.

"Detective Rankin," the guard began, "I found this fellow, he is a vendor here, behind one of the beams in the lobby. He had been attacked and knocked out."

The guard paused to explain. "I was directed to go around the park and see if anything else had happeded...after here."

The shaky vendor picked up the story after Dan, stepping aside from Ulla, looked squarely at him.

"I was in the lobby, going to pick up my next tray, peanuts I think," he paused to get his breath and to think. "I passed a man down there, holding a carton from Food Service." He paused again. "I think I remember...he looked at me and I think he followed me. I was going to look back but somebody grabbed me from behind and I could not see." He stopped. "Next thing, I was picked up," he said as he nodded to the security guard, "and my cap and jacket were gone."

Dan was eager to question the youth. "This man," he began slowly, "do you think he did this to you?"

The youth shook his head. "I don't know; I cannot say for sure."

Another question had to be put forth by Dan. "Why did you notice him in the first place?"

"Well," the vendor replied, "I guess it was because this was a night game and he was wearing such a big straw hat."

A vendor 's cap and jacket and a Food Service carton were sufficient for entrance to the Press Box.

His name was Tod Poole and he came from the rural heartland to the big city and became one of the very best sports writer of baseball. When he hired on to a writing position with a leading newspaper, he capitalized each letter of his given name, placed a period between them, pronounced each one, so the by-line of his column became T.O.D. Poole and he soon was known simply as T.O.D.. Say T.O.D. and it was known who was talked about.

However, this unique by-line was not the reason for his recognition, it was his astute knowledge of the game. Physically, he could never have been a player. He lacked the ability, was short in stature, and not strong. He did not deny his appearance though. He dressed in the natty manner of a small man, suits, fitted jackets, polished shoes. But in all aspects of the game of baseball, he was the epitome. The unqualified became the decent advocate. He studied, he knew the game and his reports were direct and honest. In a groaning statement it could be said he knew the ins and the outs of the game, but the meaning implied total understanding.

What did most for his reputation, however, was his incredible instinct for predictions. With amazing accuracy he called World Series Championship teams, most valuable players, hitting and pitching winners. Guess if you like, but follow him and you would be right. He was too good to be ignored. His opinions were sought and accepted. What does T.O.D, think? What does T.O.D. forecast?

His writings could be critical but never belligerent and he took to task so called insiders who made deals, stating that never trade a fast player for a slow one or trade a young player for an older one. His writings were unusual and with his reputation he expanded the perimeters of the game. One of his most discussed and debated stories came about when he expressed a classic description of baseball. He called it Greek tragedy which he had picked up from no less than a university professor. In Greek tragedy, each stage is expressed by actions or series of actions. So in baseball, every play consists of that: outfielders are moved about for every batter, the infield shifts. Same thing.

A second article T.O.D. wrote became equally discussed. He wrote that baseball was physical science, based on Bernoulli's theory of air pressure adjustment. He had seen a demonstration of this at the Science Museum and the principle was elevation, velocity, and pressure. Well, that is a curve ball, isn't it?

Such articles along with his knowledge and expertise stirred up resentment and envy as well as admiration. Most of these feelings came in all sorts of outbursts based on his capitalized by-line. He was called everything from That Old Dog to The Opus Dei and all imaginable monikers in between.

Now, the final t.o.d. for T.O.D. was during the last inning.

The Wrigley Field office was rightly concerned and very worried about the murders that had occurred at the park. The St. Louis Cardinals were scheduled next to meet the Cubs and such a series always was filled with high enthusiasm and emotion, a situation where anything could unexpectedly get out of hand in an already diffused atmosphere.

Detective Rankin went to Wrigley Field to discuss the situation with the anxious officials. He assured them that his office was handling the situation precisely as information was discovered and given by the crime lab. He related to them that he believed the two murders were done by one and the same person. They asked for evidence and he could hardly explain that the killer wore a straw hat and how could one pick that out in the 40,000 numbered crowds? Instead, he confessed that he had two eye witnesses that divulged an identical piece of evidence but he quickly asked them to keep this confidential at this point in the investigation. As for motive, he had none. He did not have any idea why anyone would do killing here at Wrigley Field. For why? For what cause? For what reason? He could not give any answer to that.

Detective Rankin realized that the Wrigley Field office had to make some public statement so he asked them to state their concern but of utmost importance was the safety of everyone. Security would be increased throughout the park and the Press Box and also for the players and personnel of all teams.

The St. Louis Cardinals came in as the powerful, strictly professionals, meaning they were drilled in sound and basic fundamentals that coordinated into a team and made them the ones to beat in their division.

Dan's plan was to appear at the games as a fan but without a reserved seat. Dressed in casual attire, he would walk around the park, going into all areas, being watchful of anyone or any incident that might be suspicious. He was staying close to the crime scene and hopeful that some type of break would occur in the murder investigation. The security guards and the extra police were informed of his plan and his identity and by secret signal could join him instantly in the event of any dangerous situation.

Dan started in the lower level along the box seats looking to the right and left as he passed each section. His main focus was in the clue of the straw hat; he looked anxiously for anyone wearing such a topper. The afternoon was hot and sunny and, strangely, for that area of the park there were few men wearing straws. He passed along the first base side and behind the Cardinals dugout was a group of their fans, red hat fans, and in high spirits. Nothing amiss there, Dan thought, but as he went on he heard a low moan emerge from the group but it was because the Cubs had scored the first run. Sometimes when a challenge is great, fortitude can rise and meet it as the Cubs did in taking a quick and early lead in the game.

Dan felt the thrill of the moment but he was also cautionary as he knew and remembered the Cardinals teams and they were not to be taken lightly. When Dan came to the games with his father they saw them as the "gas house gang" with unexpected plays, terror on the base paths, stealing bases, upsetting pitchers, and even sliding home, spreading dust all over. They were led by players like "Ducky" Medwick, Stan Musial, and the pitching brothers, Dizzy and Daffy Dean.

The Cubs maintained the lead after Dan had scanned the lower level and proceeded to the top. He walked slowly along the railing and carefully scrutinized the crowd below him. He took special note of straw hat wearers and tried to recognize unusual behavior. He trusted his instincts that experience had given him but he also knew that some people were pretty good actors and could feign anything.

Another inning in the game had been played but no scoring; then in the third inning, the Cardinals gained a run when their lead off hitter got a double and the next batter connected with a ground ball but it was fielded with a high throw, pulling the first baseman out of position and dribbling off into right field. Before the ball could be stopped and played, the runner on second base streacked home and the score was tied. But the Cubs refused to despair and they followed in their half of the third inning with back to back home runs and the game still in their favor at 3 to 1.

Dan had to move on and the next area for him was the upper deck. He always enjoyed this area for he had seen many games from there with his father. They were high up, so it seemed to Dan then, but he could see all around the park and the neighborhood and even the lake. His father bought him a hot dog and a root beer and about the sixth or seventh inning, he got a bag of peanut s. It was like a treasure as he pulled out each peanut separately and crumbled them to break the shell. Usually a twist at the middle would break the shell and the tiny brown nuts could be pulled out and savored in his churning jaws. Ah, the pure delights of childhood!

Every game was much the same in this respect and yet so different as they saw all the teams and the great players they had. Great players such as Warren Spahn and Eddie Mathews with Milwaukee, Mel Ott leading in the New York Giants, Sandy Koufax with the then Brooklyn Dodgers, and the Cincinnati Reds who had Johnny VanderMeer who pitched double no-hit games, two in a row. There were many other players and they all came and Dan, with his father, saw them all.

The game had continued in contentious fashion. The Cardinals came back in the fourth inning scoring another run but the Cubs refused to be threatened and scored one more run, maintaining their lead at 4 to 2.

Dan's journey through the upper deck was similar to his survey of the lower deck. Nothing was exposed that caused him concern. He went on, past the outfield to scout the citizens of the bleachers, a group unto themselves, possessing uniformity of style, appreciation of all vocal abilities in talent and decibels, and dedicated to the proposition that every man is entitled to a decent level of disrespect.

When Dan joined them the ritual chants were in progress for the sixth inning posted one more run for the Cardinals, making the score now Cubs 4, Cardinals 3, and the top of that inning was not yet over and the Cardinals continued their threat with only one out. It took five pitchers from the Cubs bull pen to put out the fire and keep any additional runs from scoring. Bedlam was rife at Wrigley Field with the bipartisan crowd but it was pure baseball. Both teams must have been exhausted after the lengthy inning and hard fought battle and no more scoring was accomplished and the Cubs claimed victory.

The second game was different. The Cardinals sent in their top pitcher, first in their rotation, and predicted to win twenty games for the year. He began his stint as if he wished to get to that number in a hurry. He held the Cubs scoreless, inning after inning, and giving up scratch hits that scarcely cleared the infield. The Cubs did manage a solid hit, a double, but the batter remained there as he could not be driven in by following batters.

The Cubs pitcher was a hopeful prospect brought up from the farm system. The rookie was good, though a bit nervous, and he held on for several innings.. Perhaps his nervousness overcame him and he lost some of his control or maybe his mechanics and style were worked out and the Cardinals scored heavily against him. The young pitcher gave up 3 runs, 2 men on base, and no outs when he left for the shower room. The cubs relief pitchers, used so much the previous day, were ineffective and allowed the two runners to score and the Cubs lost.

Dan's plan was the same as yesterday; he went through all the areas of Wrigley Field from the lower level, the upper deck, around the Press Box and media center, and onto the bleachers, but he picked up nothing that could be suspicious. He checked with the security and police details and they, too, deemed nothing as unusual or out of the ordinary. There seemed to be no evidence of any behavior that called for an investigation. The first two games then were played out in tense but high excitement in crowded Wrigley Field with no incident that could be classified as troublesome or even questionable.

However, the third game had yet to be played.

The afternoon was hot and it could be stated that the two teams got heated up also but not by the expected line-ups. The Cubs had to turn to a utility infielder to replace the regular player who had developed a hamstring injury. The substitue player was intended as a "get on base" type but instead he cleared the bases with two long outfield hits that drove in runs and gave the Cubs four runs. In one of those innings, the Cubs sent nine batters to the plate to score three of the runs. It seemed that it took a lot of players in one inning, such as pitchers one game, hitters another, for the Cubs to show any kind of effort.

Like the Cubs, the Cardinals changed their starting team. They had to use a reserve player also, replacing a hit batsman, and then this player, while playing the outfield, tore down some of the ivy when he hit the wall. During the one inning deluge by the Cubs, the Cardinals sent in a pitcher they had acquired recently in a major league trade. He was new to the team, new to the league, and new to scouting reports but he went in and got the 10th, 11th, and 12th batters out.

With all these unknown experiences occurring, it might be said that the "lesser lights" were controlling the game.

Dan got the call as he was preparing to go to the bleachers in his continued park surveillance. The call came from the upper deck which he had just left. A vendor lay at the bottom of a flight of steps. Dan felt a shock jolt when he arrived and looked down at the man sprawled at the bottom, a shattered tray of peanuts lay around him and his face was upturned in an unusual and crooked angle. The vendor was wearing a new cap and jacket that now were twisted around his head and body. To land in such a position signaled to Dan that a force was behind his fall as if he made a dive from the top.

Dan recognized the vendor as the one whose previous cap and jacket were stolen when T.O.D. was killed. What gave the shock jolt to Dan was the frightening realization that this death was intended and carried out by one person. Was the vendor killed because he had recognized this person? What frightened Dan even more was that this person had been in the ball park and perhaps Dan had seen him too when he had looked upon the crowd and the person had entered the upper deck soon after Dan had left.

"It was an accident; he tripped," came a voice in the crowd as the fans were taken to the sides and cautioned to remain still and allow the police and the medics to do their preliminary work.

"He tripped. I'm certain," came a supporting voice near the bottom step where Dan had descended for a closer examination of the body. Dan turned in the voice direction and looked upon a woman with a round face, rosy cheeks, and wearing a cap with a large visor over them and a curtain rod of thin brown curls along the neck.

"He came down those steps like a ski slope," she went on "and hit the railing right in front of me." She nodded the visored covered head toward the bloody spot where Dan had just halted. "Isn't that right, Henry?" she continued now turning toward the little man in a baseball cap seated next to her.

"Yes, dear," was his reply.

Dan looked at the woman. "You say he tripped?"

"Well, he must have," she answered quickly. "I saw him up there at the top selling peanuts and the next thing I knew he was tumbling down the aisle. I had just turned to my husband to tell him I wanted some peanuts too, Isn't that right, Henry?"

"Yes, dear," Henry answered. "I was getting the money…."

"Show him, Henry," the command came.

Henry showed where he had unzipped his trouser pocket, pulled out a wallet, and was counting the money. "It is safe," he explained.

Dan asked, "Did you see the vendor at the top?"

Henry nodded. "I saw him and a man…."

"Henry, the man asked one question. If you have anything to say tell that to the man."

"Yes, dear,"

Dan became very interested and asked, "You say you saw a man there?"

"Buying peanuts," Henry replied with an anxious look at his wife.

She shook her head at his look. "Henry, why do you ramble on and on about everything unimportant?"

"Yes, dear."

Dan continued to look at Henry. "You saw a man buying peanuts from the vendor?"

Henry did not speak, he only nodded his head.

"Can you describe the man?" Dan had to ask.

"I was getting the money...."

"Henry, you are answering questions about what? Here you are taking time, unzipping your pocket, getting your wallet, counting money while a vendor is falling down the steps and a game is going on. Do you see anything?"

"Yes, dear," Henry paused and waited for a void, then uttered, "He had a hat."

A sigh of disgust came from the woman. "Of course, Henry. Everybody wears a hat in this kind of weather."

"Yes, dear," Henry answered and breathed out, "straw."

Another disgusted sigh came forth, "Henry, I wish you would learn to concentrate. You waste people's time with all your talk."

"Yes, dear."

The final score that day was: Cubs 5; Cardinals 4. To Dan, the score at Wrigley Field was: murders 3; solutions 0.

The next morning, Dan had moved into a part of his investigation he dreaded the most, where all things seemed to be going nowhere. It gave him a lethargy that would not lift his spirits, having no leads or evidence. It did not help that he felt the oppressive heat coming to the department or even the earlier delicious breakfast Ulla had prepared for him or the cool shower he remained under for a longer time than usual. Dan was discouraged and pessimistic and it was all caused by the Wrigley Field murders. The death of the vendor the previous day had been reported as an accident, unfortunate, but an accident. It did not help that the media aided this consensus. It came about because reporters questioned many fans who told them that the vendor had tripped and fell.

Of course, this did not support Dan in what he believed and what he knew about this "accident" and the other murders, but the fact was that he was baffled. It was not the first time Dan had been caught in a similar circumstance, not understanding the situation. The circumstance went back several years and it included his own son.

No child was more wanted than Rolf and he and Ulla were ecstatic about the baby boy with soft blond hair and blue eyes who was theirs.

They reveled in Rolf's infant comeliness that got admiring glances when out, his abundant good health, and active and curious behavior. It was this behavior that first pleased them and then became overwhelming as it became exuberant and went to the extreme. Rolf was never still or inclined to stationary play but he was quick and agile and always on the move, from here to there and all over. It forced Dan to build a fence around the yard so Rolf would not run out onto the street. Ulla took Rolf to the park where there was much space for his scampering but she always dressed Rolf in a bright colored shirt so she could see him.

Dan and Ulla questioned the doctor concerning Rolf's actions but got no answer except that Rolf was a healthy and active child. Sleep was hard to come by until Dan purchased an old rocking chair and Ulla would rock Rolf back and forth for a long while until he finally slipped into slumber. By that time, Ulla was near slumber also, exhausted, and with drooping head. Trying to talk to Rolf was wasted time as he would screech and run away, but he liked music, any kind, just so it was a sound and continuous and he could hop and spin in a joyous dance. The situation was like a drive in the car, music playing, and Rolf in the back seat flaying his legs and arms, on a journey without a stop.

Still, the doctors had no advice, only assessments like "outgrow the behavior" and "will develop interests later". It was hard on Ulla. The joy and love she possessed for Rolf became mixed with worry and anxiety. She became overly concerned about all Rolf's behavior and even had Dan put a lock on the closet where he kept his policeman's gear lest Rolf hurt himself or others in some unsuspecting moment. Fatigued and distraught, she consulted the doctor also for care and would receive soothing, understanding statements like:

"So what has Rolf done today?"

And her answers would be like "he picked all the flowers out of my garden".

Mrs. Smith was hired to help Ulla, She took over most of the household chores and, being a big and strong woman, she was a bit of a challenge to Rolf's rampages. For this, Rolf liked her and the contests between them were happy and full of laughs.

With this help came a little respite for Ulla and she had been advised to find an interest of her own. She decided on a flower garden as therapy and relaxation. She enjoyed her garden, but when the results were evident, the flowers in bloom in beautiful colors and shapes, it was destroyed. Rolf was attracted to the patch and made a run for it. He knew Mrs. Smith was chasing behind him but before she caught him, he had plucked the flowers, held them high like a trophy and laughing, presented them to Mrs, Smith.

True relief for Dan and Ulla did not come until Rolf passed four years of age but still only had the language skills he had at 18 months. Dan and Ulla were referred to a specialist, new in the area, who told them that Rolf was autistic.

Autistic? Never heard of that! Dan and Ulla were stunned and unknowing. Now? What to do now? The specialist advised them to place Rolf in a special facility for treatment. They investigated the only two such facilities in the country, one in the east and the other in the southwest. They decided on the least expensive one in the southwest. This facility agreed to the application for Rolf to be brought there but their rule was no moms allowed to do so. So Ulla dressed Rolf in his nicest suit and the patent leather shoes he loved and he was ready to go with Dan. Her last words at the doorway were: "If you don't like the facility, don't leave him. Promise me, Danny."

On the plane, Rolf was thrilled by the trip, seeing clouds and sky and the flight attendants were enchanted by this happy and beautiful little boy. When they landed in the southwest, Dan and Rolf were met by two matrons from the facility. They spent time talking with Dan and showing the facility, in and around the grounds and the complete area surrrounding it. Dan got to see it all.

When Dan returned, he called Ulla from the O'Hare airport and said, "I left him."

As soon as time allowed, Dan took Ulla southwest to see the facility. Her sorrow was eased as she met the staff and was escorted around the building and grounds, She saw that Rolf was well cared for and, most pleasing and satisfying, she saw that Rolf was happy and lively with no taint of sadness.

Thereafter, Dan and Ulla made frequent trips to the facility especially for holidays and Rolf's birthday. On the latter occasions, they were permitted to bring ice cream and cake and have a party for all the fourteen boys there. The visits became less as the birth dates added over the years and the drifting emotional ties widened between Dan and Ulla and Rolf. Rolf was attached to the circle of those at the facility. The boys delighted and committed to themselves. Together they entered their own world, a little Eden, where they existed as wished, completely happy, no expressed pain or sorrow and anyone who looked upon them was an outlander with no understanding or way of coming into their fold.

The visits of Dan and Ulla also were made fewer when Ulla was carrying their second child and after baby Carol was born. The trips were too difficult at this time.When Carol was older, the three of them went to see Rolf, explaining "brother Rolf" to Carol. The meeting between the siblings was one of disquiet because of the differences between the two children. Carol was everything that Rolf had not been. She was easy to care for, loving and obedient, and so often Ulla would say to Dan, "II didn't know what it was to raise a normal child."

If such could be a problem, it was that Carol was pretty and popular. In school she was recognized for these attributes and became the girl friend of the boy from the wealthiest family. Milton was the son of an outstanding lawyer. Milton dressed well and had a car of his own. On rainy or cold days he began to drive Carol home from school. Then he took her to fancy dinners and parties where his father was speaker. Milton outlined his plans to Carol, his education was to continue at a prestigious law school in the east and he wanted to take her with him. A ring with a jewel was presented as engagement.

However, this fairy tale picture was marred by William. He was on the other side of the fence, the boy next door. He grew up with Carol, two kids who played and had fun together. When in school, William took part time work in the local grocery store, stocking shelves and bagging groceries. On the days he received salary, he and Carol would walk the two blocks to the ice cream parlor called the Igloo for cherry cokes and sometimes a movie.

One day, William leaned over the fence and said to Dan, "Mr. Rankin, may I have your permission to marry Carol?" Seeing the surprised look on Dan's face, he went on, "I'm getting a scholarship...in engineering...at a technical school and I have a job lined up."

This bombast from William completely floored Dan and Ulla. They did not know what to do, they discussed it with bewilderment, and decided that Carol ought to decide for herself. However, they could see that she was troubled also. With their parental concern for what would be the best for their daughter, Dan and Ulla wondered how they could be of help.

Finally, Ulla made the decision. She had planted her now forever garden and sent two empty seed packets to Carol. The packets were labeled: MARIGOLD OR SWEET WILLIAM.

Flowers send messages and it might have been a good floral year for William for Carol married him. William had his scholarship and the job he had was with a new start-up company in Hawaii. Besides all this studying and "starting up", William had to build their own house, fortunately small and in a very moderate climate. They had a son, Billy, Jr., and Dan and Ulla were sent pictures and descriptions of their grandson. Billy, Jr. did not have the fair looks of Rolf but rather brown hair and eyes. Nevertheless, Dan and Ulla were well pleased and said that was all right too. So their trips then continued, to the southwest to see Rolf and then on to Hawaii to see Billy Jr. Two boys in their life, each at a distance and yet so close to them.

Another day and Dan's discouragement with the investigation was not diminished. No leads had come in and the forensic studies of the Wrigley Field parking lot, the press box and the tier of seats where the vendor died brought no information or clues from any scene.

When investigations seem to go no where as now, Dan usually came to the conclusion that the situation required different thinking and taking another turn. If no evidence was present, it must be apparent in some other way.

Then the letter came.

It was brought to him by Scooter.

"For you, sir," he said as he handed it to Dan. For a moment, both of them stared at the crude piece of mail. The envelope had no return signature and the postal date indicated it was a local letter and addressed to RANKIN at the department address.

"Shall I stay, sir?" Scooter asked, revealing an uneasiness when odd posts of any kind come to the department.

"If you wish, Scooter," Dan replied, uneasy himself, as he slit the envelope open and withdrew one sheet of paper and laid it open on his desk. Both he and Scooter read the message without comprehension. Printed words and letters from newspapers were cut out and pasted on the sheet of paper. The lines and letters were uneven and it read:

Look out

The EXPOS BeCAme

The Nationals

BRo

Dan and Scooter were speechless. Whatever did it mean? It was a mention of two baseball teams, the BRo was short for brother, and the opening salutation was a threat. The message gave nothing of identification, the stationery was the general kind purchased anywhere and the letters could he cut from any newspaper.

"What do you think, sir?" Scooter asked at last.

Dan shook his head and answered, "I don't know. I just don't know." He paused to reflect and then added, "Somehow it means something for our investigation. It has to be the only connection. But how and why?"

Scooter shrugged his shoulders, unable to offer any bit of information. He could only repeat Dan's words, "I don't know either, sir," Left with that, he turned and went back to his desk.

Dan stayed at his desk with the message before him. He read it over and over again hoping that something would be revealed therein about the murders. In all his experience he knew that seldom were cases simple or easy. Once a case was presented it seemed that a kind of barrier went around it and limited the scrutiny and extent of the study of what had happened. Often, in such a time, some minor truth escaped or went unnoticed. All one can do is work within those barriers and if that minor truth should come it must be in it's own way.

Dan looked at the words, read them, compared them, until they seemed to stare back at him, steadfast and challenging. He blinked,

58

his vision quickened, and then he saw it. The letters gave it up. After reading so long, he realized what he had read. It came to him in the word BeCAme. It was one word with three capital letters: BCA or to put them in order: ABC.

Suddenly, he sat upright and his body tensed. It was what he already knew about the Wrigley Field murders. The teams the Cubs played against at these times were the Astros, the Brewers, and the Cardinals.

Quickly, he called out to Scooter. "Scooter, check the schedule. What is the next team to play the Cubs?"

In a moment, Scooter answered, "The Dodgers".

Ah, Dan was up beat and excited; he got the message: since there was no E named team, the next and final killing would be during the Dodger series. But the "who" and the "why" were the questions now. Dan faced these questions but now they filled him with exhileration because they gave him a step on the offense. A slight corner had been lifted in the investigation but it was enough to give him a beginning, a small but important half-step to finding the solution. This crude and simple message was a gauntlet thrown down to him by the killer and Dan knew his challenge was to find and stop him.

The forensic labs had not come to Dan with any information but now he could go to them with a piece of his own for them to evaluate. The post mark on the envelope indicated that it was a local letter. The forensics could trace that mark to the mail box where the letter had been dropped. When given the address of the location, Dan lost no time. An excited Scooter joined him and they sped away and found the mail box. The mail box was located on the corner in front of the Vietnamese grocery store which was boarded up after the robbery and the owner slain a few months ago.

They both stood silently for a moment, looking at the forlorn,and closed building and then looked at each other , seeing puzzlement in each other. Without a word, Dan returned to the car and Scooter followed. Inside, Scooter asked, "What do we do now, sir?" as they drove away and headed back to the department.

Dan was deliberating and gave his answer to Scooter's question. "We go back and review everything we know about this case, beginning with the surveillance tape."

In his office, Dan set up the tape, this time in slow motion as he wanted to study every nuance, every movement that transpired. It began an eerie drama as the three masked gun men entered the store with guns drawn. Their steps were slow and careful as they came forward. It became a "danse macabre" of ghastly grace as the men's arms and hands moved into position and their bodies stepped around as dancers on cue. Their postures whirled and dodged at the rise of the Vietnamese, a clear dark head from behind the counter and his arms lifting aloft the shot gun. Heads now were down and up, trying to avoid the weapons aimed at them. A shelf fell easily and the flying bottles were set off like cascades of light flares around the scene. Then, one head bent lowly, rose up and his left arm raised over it and the hand pointed the gun at the Vietnamese. It was the last jolt against the grocer as his moving arms lifted high and his large gun fell from them as he bent back and tumbled behind the counter. The tape ran out; it was over.

Dan had seen an important clue: a left handed gun man had shot the owner.

Other information Dan had on the case was the tip a bystander had provided on the car used by the burglars and it led Dan and a homicide squad to an abandoned house on the outskirts along a county road. The raid caught only one of the robbers there. He was trapped and a shootout followed and the robber was slain. Dan placed a surveillance car on the house, believing that if it was the hide out for the gang, the other two members might return. Such an event did not occur, however, and the police surveillance was withdrawn after a considerate time.

Now Dan wanted to go back there, review the scene a he had done the tape and, perhaps, discover something missed or unexpected from before. Caution was necessary, he knew, in the event that his belief was true and the two gun men had returned there. He assembled his homicide squad again, took Scooter, and made for the old house.

As they approached, the desolation was stark, there was no sign of life around the place, no vehicle, no indication of heavy traffic on the road, and the house itself was in decay. Nothing new in Dan's vision, it was the same scene as previous; but he remembered there had been an armed gun man inside.

He led the way to an unhinged door, pushed it aside and stepped into the quiet barrenness of the place. Scooter and the others followed, all ears attuned for any noise from anywhere. They went into empty rooms, but there was no sign of any residence, sleeping, eating, and all else. Dan went ahead to the area of what had been kitchen, now open shelves on a wall, a few cabinets empty with their doors hanging loose.

The room where the one robber had been trapped and slain was an enclosed room beyond. Dan went there, stepped inside and halted in his tracks. A board was nailed to one wall and the first thing he saw hanging there, not seen before, was a straw hat. Along side was a photograph and a newspaper clipping. Dan went first to the photograph and it struck Dan to the heart; it was a picture of him and T.O.D. Poole together. It came about when T.O.D., with his erudition and sense of an unusual story, discovered that Wrigley Field became so named in 1926 and he enlisted the aid of the TV camera man to do a documentary film on 80 years of history of Wrigley Field.

Dan got into the picture, so to speak, when T.O.D. , knowing Dan as a full fledged, qualified baseball fan, requested an interview on his recollections, and rememberances of times at Wrigley Field. Dan expressed it all in compelling detail and T.O.D. loved it, printed it, and publicized it on camera, calling Dan number one fan. And so the photograph was made.

Dan blinked and turned away to the newspaper clipping and read the story:

> "One gunman in the robbery and murder of the Vietnamese grocer was caught and slain in an abandoned house on old county road. The raid was led by <u>Homicide Detective Daniel Rankin,</u> but two suspects remain at large."

Dan's name was underlined. He had not moved or spoken out to the others but remained still until Scooter came up behind him.

"Sir?" Scooter asked anxiously, then he looked before him and saw what Dan had seen. "Sir,....what?"

"I know it now, Scooter," Dan answered. "I am the target, the reason for the murders at Wrigley Field."

Dan had been under siege before, but it was a loving kind of siege because it had to do with Ulla's cooking.

Ulla made fruit soup. It consisted of plums, prunes, figs, raisins, other dried fruits, and a stick of cinnamon. These ingredients were all cooked together, then the cinnamon stick removed, were served in bowls, usually for dessert. It affected the nether regions but made for a clear complexion. It was consumed all year round: hot in the winter and cold in the summer. Dan said it was the Viking in her, feeding him fruit soup.

The siege ended when Dan purchased a book for Ulla entitled "The Culinary Art of Scandinavian Bland Cooking" or white cooking. The tide turned but now Dan was caught in the clutches of another sort: snow blinded cooking. It was good spirits food, unpretentious, but designed to provide the white in all possible forms of cooking. All vegetables could be creamed: peas, corn, broccoli, cauliflower bits, and potatoes. Others could be made pleasing by peeling: such as radishes, cucumbers, zucchini, and apples, potatoes included here also. The list went on to a staggering menu like rice pudding, tapioca pudding, cottage cheese, egg nog, cream, milk, egg coffee, cod fish, potato sausage, soda crackers, pickled herring, great northern beans, marzipan,cream puffs, pears, bread pudding, bananas, buttermilk, pea soup (yellow peas), angel food cake, vanilla frosting, mashed potatoes, white gravy, meringue, Milnot, coleslaw,Cool Whip, Reddi Whip, coconut, sour cream, divinity, creametts, cloud berries, cream of mushroom soup, marshmallow, salt, sugar, white pepper, a la mode, sugar donut holes, whipping cream, powdered sugar, and etc.

Dan always was ready to accept an invitation or go out with a group for BBQ ribs or one of those jumbo hot dogs with sauerkraut and jalepeno peppers. Yet, Dan had to admit that, all in all, he was a pretty healthy bloke.

It had been a long home stand for the Cubs, but they would be going on a road trip, hoping to go over .500 after the Dodgers series. But within this three game series was Rolf's thirtieth birthday and it made for a dilemma with Dan. His calculations of another killing during this time made the series critical. Yet, he felt an agonizing sorrow to have to forgo Rolf's birthday. He talked with Ulla, of course, but not all the details of his calculations. He told her of the impending danger at Wrigley Field and she realized this after the previous murders, but in no way could he tell her that he was the target now.

The observance of Rolf's birthday, however, was another matter which was resolved by an unexpected telephone call from Hawaii. Carol had called with two bits of happy news. First, she and William were expecting another child and second, they would all be returning to the States by early next year. William's business had gone from "upstarting" to expansion and he was promoted to General Manager to set up offices in the mid-west. He was to establish the business and hire staff and prepare for the marketing. All this made for Dan to suggest that a trip to Hawaii could be postponed now. He mentioned this to Carol and she was understanding and acceptable and thought that William would be also. Then Dan went on, "May I talk to Billy?"

Before Carol spoke a hurried farewell, she was interrupted by a light, excited voice, "Grandpa!"

"Hi, Billy," Dan greeted him quickly, "How are you?"

"I'm okay," Billy answered.

"I just talked to your Mom and she told me about your moving back here. That's great!"

"Yes, it's great!" Billy agreed in a still excited voice. "We'll be living close to you and Grandma."

Dan went on, "Well for that reason I don't think Grandma and I will come to see you now. We will wait until next year to be together and it will be fun. Okay?"

"Okay, Grandpa," Billy agreed.

Again, Dan talked to Ulla and said, in effect, that if they were not going to Hawaii should they cancel the trip to the southwest also? She sighed and remained in a quiet moment. Then, perhaps after all these years and seeing Rolf moving further away from long remembrances, it was not too difficult for her to agree with Dan.

Dan contacted the Wrigley Field office to schedule a conference concerning security. He requested that the entire staff all hired personnel and security guards be there and also the two amiable TV broadcasters, Larry and Joe. Dan told them the whole story. He presented all the facts he had gathered about the previous murders, the link to the grocery store murder, and that his current theory that another murder was to be carried out during the series with the Dodgers. The group was aghast when he told them point blank that he believed he was the target. Someone was coming to Wrigley Field to kill him. Why, they wondered, was he designated for that here and with a baseball game in progress? He could not answer that but he asked for their utmost cooperation and that his theory was valid. He went on to explain his strategy. He was enlisting a task force of police to join the security guards and be placed all around Wrigley Field, at every gate and section of the seating stands. It was a veritable net around Wrigley Field. He himself planned to he visible at all times to draw attention to him. Everyone would be equipped with phones for immediate contact with any authority. He asked the field camera men and Larry and Joe in their broadcast to report anything suspicious. Dan stressed to all of them to avoid panic and give no indication that an alert had been organized.

So Dan set forth his plan and, as said, the games could begin.

The Dodgers came in to Wrigley Field on a long winning streak. They had an effective pitching rotation and good defense which was winning games for them. These victories continued when they won the first two games of the series.

Nothing of Dan's plan, however, had occurred, nothing suspicious, no one under particular scrutiny, nothing of unusual behavior of any kind.

The third game was ready to begin and started much as the previous two: the weather remained hot but 40,000 fans entered the park for the final game. They were an eager and flamboyant crowd, their boos, catcalls, and applause erupted as each lineup was called out and the umpires got the unanimous gust of fan disapproval.

The excitement subsided into a mode of frustration when the Dodgers took an early lead of 2 - 0 by the third inning. The Cubs came back with 1 run in the fourth. The Dodgers responded with 2 runs in the fifth, making the score 4 - 1. Still fighting, the Cubs got two runs of their own in the sixth inning, bringing the score to 4 - 3 in favor of the Dodgers. Such was the game: the Cubs trying to get a break but always remaining one run behind.

By the seventh inning, the game continued with the same score but was more intense and Dan was feeling an intensity of his own. Nothing untoward had happened or was reported around the park. Had he been wrong? Was his idea and plan a mistake? His thoughts now were that he had to prove he was right. He went to the broadcasting booth and asked Larry and Joe if he could be seen while singing "Take Me Out to the Ballgame"? The announcers were taken back by his request, but they were aware of the critical situation. They already had a local basketball coach lined up to sing the lovable, adinfinitum theme song, but they quickly announced he would be joined in a surprise duet with his friend, Detective Dan Rankin. The basketball coach was indeed so surprised he began singing off key and Dan tried to cover with his basso profundo and the astonished organist played louder and a bit faster so all three ended at a different time. For Dan, this appearance had achieved his goal: the killer saw him, knew what he looked like, and where he was. Dan's silent thought now was to the killer: make your move.

The eighth inning came and went and the status quo remained. So did the first of the ninth inning with the Dodgers holding on to their lead. The last inning, the last chance, thought Dan as he continued his visible walk around the park. Where and who was the one?

This thought was so heavy upon him that he did not realize that he had been bumped in his arm. It could have been the congestion of people moving in the aisle until he saw a man stop just ahead of him. Dan stopped also and noted the man's appearance: white sneakers, brown trousers, and short sleeved shirt. When the man stopped, he lowered his head and moved his glance sideways toward Dan. Dan was stunned but became instantly aware and alert. The man moved on and Dan decided to prove his suspicions of him. Dan turned away and went up the steps in the next aisle. He halted mid-way when he spotted the man, who evidently had taken the steps up in the next aisle, was moving back and stood up ahead in front of Dan. The man made the same motion: he lowered his head but now turned it directly and gave Dan a quick look.

Dan realized the move was deliberate,the man was leading him on, he wanted Dan to follow him. Dan kept his eyes on him but fell in line and tailed after him.

The Dodgers had finished their half of the ninth inning and the Cubs began their part of the inning as the first batter flied out.

Dan had to make a move and quickly. He took the first steps that went down to beneath the stands and out of the way of crowds. The lower level was not as busy as usual as most refreshment stands had closed and most of the people there were going to the rest rooms.

Dan went immediately to the police unit stationed there and nodded to them. They waited on alert as they saw the legs with white sneakers and brown trousers descend the stairs. The police had him and Dan faced him and said, "Bro?"

The man laughed and answered, "Not me."

"Then where is he?" Dan countered quickly.

The man laughed again and replied, "For you to find out."

"I will find him out and for the killing of the Vietnamese grocer," Dan retorted.

"If he doesn't do the killing first," the man answered in like retort. "I was showing you the way."

"What's his reason?" Dan went on. "Me?"

The man nodded. "You killed his brother. Now, number one baseball fan, his plan is to kill you here before 40,000 of these fans. Big story for the reporters in the newspapers and TV."

"Why the vendor?" Dan asked quickly.

"Because he recognized Bro following you so he had to be pushed out of the way."

Dan became angry but there was no time for more interrogation of this man. Yet Dan knew he was the second man in the grocery store robbery and killing so he ordered him taken in. The police searched the man and started to lead him away when Dan said suddenly, "Hold it.!" He noticed that the mans shirt pocket opened when his arms were pulled back to be cuffed. Dan reached into the pocket and pulled out the ticket stub for the game. The ticket stub was for a section in the lower level and Dan was struck with fear as he realized that was the section he had commanded to Scooter. Dan had to move fast, he knew, and he approached that section from below where he was and then made his way up the steps.

He heard a roar from the crowd. The Cubs had sparked a ninth inning rally with a single and a stolen base.

Dan saw Scooter at the top of the section and he called him without delay. "Scooter," he said quickly, "he is in this section. Watch, be careful, but wait for my signal to act." He heard Scooter gasp and say, "Yes," and then saw him tense and move closer to the section railing. Dan looked at the ticket stub to see the location of the seat. He saw the vacant chair along the aisle but in the next seat was a young boy. Dan had expected to see the killer there and realized what happened. The two men had purchased tickets in the same section but <u>different</u> seats. Killer Bro was in another seat in that section.

The fans were excited and started a steady clapping of hands to keep the rally going as the Cubs had a runner on second and only one out. The next batter was showing his patience as he kept hitting more and more foul balls and having a count on him of 3 balls and 2 strikes. Then he finally drew a walk which put another runner on first. The decision was on the next batter. The two runners must be advanced to third and second base but should he bunt or hit to move the runners along? The batter took a few swings and then the runners were off as he laid down a perfect sacrifice bunt. Runners on second and third but two outs and Cubs trailing 4 - 3.

Dan was frantically looking over the crowd, hoping for any sign or movement by the killer. He saw nothing but he could not give up his searching. The killer was there, somewhere. Dan looked back and forth, up and down each row but no sign of anything suspicious. The movement was slow, but Dan saw it. Above, on an aisle seat by the stairs a man slowly raised a scorecard from his lap and moved something under it that reflected a quick wink of silver metal. Dan started up the stairs, placing himself directly in the center and in harm's way but he knew he could not get to the top in time to avoid being hit.

The Cubs had a chance now and they sent in a pinch hitter, one with a fairly good record as they needed a hit. The pinch hitter was a veteran player but he had experience and knowledge of what he would face in the batter's box. He took the first pitch for a called strike and then stepped out of the box for a moment of hesitation for himself and to break the concentration of the pitcher.

Dan was not close enough to the man to grab him but Scooter was just above at the railing. Dan signaled to him as he pointed out the man. Scooter came around and made for the man as Dan called out, "left hand'." and Scooter lunged for the man's arm and held as Dan reached them both.

The pinch hitter was back in the box and his next swing sent a foul ball into the section where Scooter and Dan had converged on the killer. The foul ball made the crowd stand up and scamper madly about over chairs and each other. In the broadcast booth, Larry and Joe and a camera had caught the action and, knowing the situation and seeing Dan involved, Larry and Joe quickly reported that "a couple of fellows were fighting over the foul ball".

The pinch hitter socked a clean hit to the outfield, the two runs scored and the Cubs won!!!

The crowd was wild and happy, standing on their feet and shouting with joy and paying no attention to the two men leading another man down and away.

"Grandpa, I've got two sisters!" came the light, unbelieving voice of Billy, Jr.

Dan laughed to himself but said, "That is good news, Billy, and when you come here to live, we can all be together and have some good times."

"We're going to the baseball games!" replied Billy, still excited.

"That is what we are going to do," Dan answered.

Dan had talked with Carol just before and knew about the twin girls added to their familly and also that plans were definite that they would move to the States at the beginning of the year. This thrilled Dan and he said "good times" to Carol also and then asked if Billy could go to the baseball games with him and Ulla, acknowledging that William would be very occupied establishing the business while Carol would be busy also with moving arrangements and resettling all the while caring for the twins, and consulting with a local architectural firm about plans for their new house…and so could he and Ulla have some time with Billy…

Carol consented readily, agreeing with all of Dan's observations about their immediate future; but Dan privately believed that Carol consented so that he and Ulla could enjoy the childhood of a little boy.

After the conversation, Dan went shopping. He purchased a little Cubs shirt for Billy, a new cap for Ulla in the blue color he always thought matched her eyes, and a new hat for himself, one of those fisherman's type with a small brim.

A new baseball season was starting and tickets would go on sale soon and Dan would make certain he would get them. When the day came, the three of them would don their new finery and head for Wrigley Field. They would go through the turnstiles, then up the stairs, and the scene was open before them. The field laid out in specific and cared for dimensions. He would tell Billy that it was a diamond, A DIAMOND, with facets of an infield and outfield, and he would explain all the positions and how they were played on that field. Billy would see and Billy would know.

He would tell Billy about other teams to come here and they would have great players. He would name them just as his father had done for him. The game was baseball, let others call it the national pastime, Greek tragedy, Bernoulli's theory, but baseball was it's own game, and presented on hallowed ground. Dan thought it might be a while, maybe years, for Billy to understand the last, but he would come to know that this was hallowed ground.